T0196021

AuthorHouse™ UK
1663 Liberty Drive
Bloomington, IN 47403 USA
www.authorhouse.co.uk
UK TFN: 0800 0148641 (Toll Free inside the UK)
UK Local: 02036 956322 (+44 20 3695 6322 from outside the UK)

Because of the dynamic nature of the Internet, any web addresses or links contained in this book may have changed since publication and may no longer be valid. The views expressed in this work are solely those of the author and do not necessarily reflect the views of the publisher, and the publisher hereby disclaims any responsibility for them.

Any people depicted in stock imagery provided by Getty Images are models, and such images are being used for illustrative purposes only.
Certain stock imagery © Getty Images.

This book is printed on acid-free paper.

ISBN: 979-8-8230-8582-3 (sc)
ISBN: 979-8-8230-8581-6 (e)

Print information available on the last page.

Published by AuthorHouse rev. date: 01/31/2024

authorHOUSE®

MY

ADVENTURE

TO THE

AMAZON

RAINFOREST

CONTENTS

ABOUT THE AUTHOR

Tanvi is a typical 11 year old, a painfully camera shy near-teen, an avid reader, a fussy eater and a Ms. know-it-all. Much to her parent's dismay, she also consumes an astonishing amount of chocolate and screen time.

Currently a resident of Guildford, Surrey in the UK, Tanvi has classic "start everything enthusiastically and then leave is half way" syndrome. This book is perhaps the very first finished output which has come with its fair share of tears, tantrums and threats.

The love for books, stationary and written word started early on and with the start of "creative writing" in school, she was dabbling with stories of her own. A champion at spinning tales, Tanvi started this book towards the end of primary school and now finally, it's ready !!!

Follow Tanvi as she takes you down the twisted overgrowth of the Amazon Rainforest in a personal quest for truth.

CHAPTER 1

I woke to the sound of two people talking in loud animated voices outside my bedroom door. Rubbing the sleep out of my still-shut eyes, I crawled out of bed and trudged to the door, easing it open.

Dad was telling mum he was going to the amazon rainforest for a research project for his job for 2 years and that it was too dangerous for us to go with him.

Mum was protesting vehemently, hence the argument and escalated voices. He already had two suitcases in his hand ready to go.

That was the last time I ever saw my dad.

After dad had left, I sat down beside my weeping mum and placed a comforting arm around her shoulder. "Don't worry mum, I'm here… shh shh shhh". I rocked her back and forth till she stopped heaving and shaking against me.

I stood up to get her a glass of water when a thought struck me. Dad had gone to the amazon rainforest for a research project, right? Well, all year 13's having zoology as their major subject go on a school trip with a group of highly trained explorers and teachers to the Amazon rainforest as a part of their project work and for me, year 13 was only 2 years away. I made up my mind to choose the subjects that would lead me down that path.

"I'd get you back dad" I vowed.

CHAPTER 2

Back to the present

ummmm….!" I call down the stairs. "Could you get me a torch for the trip? Pleeeease." I add because I know mum is a strong believer in magic words.

"Sure thing, sweetie." Mum replied and soon after I heard a loud thump as she closed the door behind her.

"Ok. Now that Mum was gone, I could plan how I would get away from the rest of the class to find Dad." I thought. After several agonising minutes and many false starts later what I came up with was this: I would tell the teacher that I needed to go to the toilet. Then, instead of making my way straight back, I would sneak away into the rainforest with my backpack which I would have put in the bushes earlier that day. If anyone saw me and questioned my whereabouts, I would say that I had lost my way back to the campsite.

Foolproof, right?

Now back to packing. I hurriedly threw everything into my waterproof backpack:

Water filtering bottle
Foldable walking stick
Mosquito net
Sleeping bag
Deet - Insect repellent
Foot balm
Compass
Illustrated guide to the rainforest
Pencils and a sketch pad
Binoculars

The only missing item from my list was the torch which mum was buying.

"All set." I thought "All set!'

CHAPTER 3

After Mum came back, I stuffed the torch in my already full bag. Mum had insisted I sleep early for the journey tomorrow so I got under the covers quickly.

Alas! Sleep eluded me.

I had a restless night as I was sick with nerves, thinking of all the ways my plan could go wrong.

"What if they ask what I am doing with a backpack if I were on my way to the toilet? Or what if I forgot where I had put my backpack and started to wander about like an idiot?"

Dreading these scenarios, I finally drifted off into a fitful, dreamless sleep.

Let me ask you a question.

"How would you feel if you were in my shoes?"

"Yeah! You would be feeling low and miserable just like how I was. But, you DO understand it was essential for me to complete this mission otherwise I would forever feel guilt for not fulfilling my resolve."

Today

I woke up with a jolt and quickly got dressed. I made my bed and flung open the door. I ran into my mum's bedroom, yelling "RISE AND SHINE!" at the top of my lungs.

'Ughhh, it's too early!" She muttered, rolling over so that her back was to me. I tried to rouse her once again but when she used a pillow to cover her ears it was clear that she was still asleep and not willing to wake up just yet.

"Fine! I'll make my own breakfast. See you downstairs in 10!"

I rushed downstairs and almost collided with the dining table. Grabbing the edge for support and I just about managed to stop myself from falling flat on the floor. Phew!

Taking a deep breath and then pouring some milk to go with my cereal, I did a mental check list of my plan. Mum still hadn't come downstairs, so upon finishing, I hurried upstairs to fetch my bag and to check on her. She was just about ready.

"Where are you, Mum?"

"Coming Flora."

That's me. My name is Flora Maxwell. Short for Florence Indigo Maxwell.

"Today's the school trip and I'm not missing it for the world. Quick mum, we have got to get going.....!"

Mum walked out of her room and followed me downstairs. "I see you have had breakfast." She smiled at me warmly. "Well, done."

TANVI SHARMA

I put on my waterproof hiking boots and rain mac, and with the rucksack on my back I followed Mum to the bus stop where we waited for the school bus to arrive.

CHAPTER 4

I spotted my bestie heading towards class so I ran up to her and gave her a high five.

"Hey."

"Hey Flora."

"Are you excited?" I asked.

"Yup. Even more because I know you are coming." Millie replied.

Guilt consumed me.

Millicent was my best friend and I knew that she was only coming for this trip because I was going even if she didn't say or show it. Being the nerd she was, Millie was happier behind a computer screen doing data analytics and preparing project reports than she was running around doing field work.

It was time for a calculated risk.

"Hey Mill." I said, "You know about my dad being a researcher, right?"

"Uhhuh", she nodded absently.

".. and you know he's travelling for his research, right?"

"Well… Now I do."

I took a deep breath that made her stop and look at me quizzically.

"I made a vow to myself 2 years ago when he left that I would one day, find him. One thing you must know is that his research project was based in the Amazon and that is where we are headed so…"

Suddenly the smile on Millicent's face vanished. Pulling me to one side she fixed my eyes in a cold, hard stare.

"Oh no no no. Florence Indigo Maxwell. You listen to me now. Please don't do what I think you are going to do and please don't drag me into it."

I knew she meant it. She always means it when she calls me by my full name.

"We'll cross the bridge when we get to it." Is just about all I could manage to squeeze out of my mouth.

*

We got on the coach from Brasilia to Manoa, the base camp from where most expeditions to the rainforest began.

I would have sat with Millie. Obviously! But today she went and sat with Fiona Groves the most popular girl in the school, so I turned my gaze away from them and sat down near the back. I guess I couldn't really blame her, she must be fuming.

The journey took hours but we finally arrived. Holy guacamole! Let the adventure begin!

CHAPTER 5

Basecamp

I was blown away.

I had never before seen such natural beauty, there was green everywhere. This was such a contrast to the busy city life in Brasilia. As the other classmates filtered out of the coach behind me, gasps of delight filled the atmosphere around. I didn't blame them, not one bit! I had been waiting for this moment for so long yet nothing could have possibly prepared me for it. No books, no videos and no pictures could compare the actual experience.

There were just too many things to take in, I didn't know where to look first. My brain went into a freeze for a second; forgetting to breathe, speak or move. Slowly as I regained control and composure over my senses; feeling like a child in Disneyland, high on a bucket full of candyfloss; this felt like a dream realised.

The canopy towered over the rainforest as the forest floor buzzed with excitement. The range of colours were a whole other topic. The trees varied from neon to olive greens whilst the flowers came in all shades of red, blue, yellow, purple and pink. This was a sight to sore eyes.

Staring at this spectacle of nature with wide eyed wonder, I almost forgave Dad but then remembering the sinking feeling of abandonment, I pushed that thought out of my mind.

The class radiated outwards, some with their drawing book and pencils out, some people already flashing their camera lights at the flora and fauna. When the teachers eventually quietened the pupils, the explorers had already found a safe place and set up camp for the night.

"Settle down everyone. Here is the printed copies of the itinerary and a map for tomorrow."

One of the students in our group handed them out. I looked down at mine:

The Amazon rainforest takes its name from the Amazon River, which spans the borders of eight South American countries -- Brazil, Peru, Bolivia, Ecuador, Colombia, Venezuela, Suriname, Guyana and French Guiana. Amazon rainforest camping entices seasoned campers with the promise of an exhilarating adventure, but the experience requires meticulous preparation in order to ensure your own safety. Rainforest camping techniques bear close resemblance to camping methods elsewhere, but the possibility of exposure to malaria, typhoid and other illnesses is greater in the Amazon. Take extra precautions against potential health issues.

It then went down to listing a list of Do's and Don'ts.

I couldn't help noticing that there was an emphasis on the DON'Ts.

"We leave at the break of dawn", the teacher continued.

Hugging myself in the anticipation of my own little adventure that lay ahead or perhaps it was the quiet chill that had descended over our camp; I whispered to myself, "This is it."

I might have been louder than I thought because the next thing I knew Millie had me cornered again.

"Flora." She spoke in a dangerously calm manner. "I knew you wouldn't listen to me but I'm coming with you no matter what. I know I said previously not to drag me into it, but for better or worse, we're better off as a team, watching each other's backs."

I let out a breath that I didn't know I was holding.

"Oh my God... you're the best friend anyone could ask for. Thank you, thank you, thank you."

"That's enough, you silly oaf" she said, "now let go of my hand before you squish it to pulp!"

We clambered into our sleeping bags, but we didn't actually sleep, we just pretended to; I ran Millie through my plan and we were going to put it into action as soon as possible.

*

4 am. The still of night. A beautiful harmony that was the sound of the rainforest.

All too soon there was sounds of stirrings, yawns and stretches. Sleeping bags being rolled up, camp fires being put out, one team getting on with preparing and packing a simple breakfast to be put in everyone's backpack whereas one team tidying the campsite.

Everyone was dressed in quick dry clothing, full pants and tops as well as long wellies or hiking boots.

Then, everyone rose simultaneously. I was the only one still sitting. Was it nerves? A sudden fear?

"Come on Flora. Chop chop", said the teacher clapping her hands together.

Everyone gathered their belongings. We had a quick headcount, maps and binoculars in hand, and the team was ready to hike.

The teacher had put us in two separate groups. Each of the groups was to be accompanied by 2 teachers and 2 explorers. Each group had 19 members; adults included. Millie and I were in different groups; everything was falling into place.

'Any final questions?' the teacher asked.

I put my hand up. "Yes?" she said.

"Please may I go to the toilet? I'll join up with the other group."

"Sure."

In the background I could hear Millie asking the same thing and getting the same answer.

Pivoting on the spot, I hurried towards the toilets until I was out of sight. From the corner of my eye, I thought I saw Fiona emerge from the same direction and as she passed me, I felt her stare, but I was on high to get going. I broke into a run. When I arrived at the toilets, I found Millie already there crouching in between the leaves and bracken. Backpacks were retrieved from behind the bushes and slung on.

"Ready?" I said.

"Ready." She answered. And we were off.

CHAPTER 6

We ran.

We ran until we were out of breath. We ran until our lungs burned for air. We ran until our legs quivered and refused to hold us up. We ran until we could run no further.

It was me who stopped first.

Doubling over, as my lungs took a moment to fill up with air, breathlessly I said "Do you think we are far enough from the camp now? You think they might have already noticed we are not in either of the groups?"

"Uhhhhhhhhh … honestly, I don't know. I'm hoping they won't notice till the end of day when they return from their hike. Let's keep walking a bit more now and put more distance between us. We can find some clearing to set the tent up. I think it might be best if we get a fire going then and we can plan our next move as we eat." Millie replied, panting.

*

The Amazon Rainforest is naturally a home to the world's unique and most diverse plant and animal species. The rainforest is oozing with biodiversity because more than 60,000 species of plants and trees can be found here.

As we walked through this beautiful ecosystem, our senses heightened and alive, we began to notice the hidden treasures we were fortunate to witness.

"Oh, look there!" I gasped, pointing to a nearby flower. "The nymphaea plant. My favourite."

The delicate petals were white. Pearly white. Towards the centre was a hint of baby pink and the absolute middle was a beautiful orangey gold. The flower petals had a lovely velvety texture that felt soothing to the fingers and the fascinating species were perfectly harmless.

"Did you know..." began Millie.

"I know everything about this particular species", I snapped, hurt at the thought that she would say such a thing about my favourite flower.

"... that the nymphaea flower got its name from the nymphs of Greek and Latin mythology?"

"Oh. Actually, I didn't know that." I whispered, feeling embarrassed.

"Don't worry." She said, slapping me on my back.

"Owwwww! What was that for?"

"Just like that Ms. I-know-everything." She laughed, choosing not to answer my question.

We saw some interesting plants: heliconia and trillium but whilst they were pretty, they were not as fascinating to me as the nymphaea plant.

A sudden yowl distracted us from our conversation. Instantly, we turned our heads to witness an incredible animal. The ocelot.

For the uninitiated with rainforest wildlife, the ocelot is a spotted wild cat, medium-sized and it weighs between 8 and 15.5 kg. Thankfully, it preys on small terrestrial mammals, such as armadillos and possums. Both male and female become mature at around two years of age though they can breed throughout the year. The females give birth to one to three kittens after carrying them for 2-3 months.

This one looked like she was guarding a nesting site with 2 small kittens.

"Back away slowly." Millie whispered. "We do NOT want it to chase us. We should be grateful it's protecting it's young so perhaps it won't leave its nesting site if it doesn't have to. It has to be in breeding season from the sound of that yowl."

One foot after the other, we retreated from the scene.

Once we were far away, enough for us to let out our breath, we started walking normally.

We trekked on, ducking under the coiling vines hanging overhead, using our walking sticks to get the really low foliage out of our way, talking about our close encounter with such a rare species. Eventually, we emerged at a clearing.

We heard it before we saw it. It started off as a slow murmur but soon it was a loud roaring sound, so loud we probably needed to shout to each other to hear ourselves. Thankfully, the view was so ethereal, we could all but …. stare.

Amidst the undergrowth, was a magnificent waterfall leading to a majestic, snaking river. The Amazon River. The waterfall hit the rocks with extraordinary force, sending tremors through the water.

I gaped at the glorious scene.

"I…I…I think we are far enough from the rest of the class to set up camp for the night here."

I stole a glance towards Millie. She was also just standing there, mouth open, staring at the water.

"I do suppose you're right." She replied. She nudged me and I followed her gaze as it lingered at a spot between the waterfall and the rocks behind it. It took me a moment to realise what she was looking at.

"O M G." I blurted like an idiot. "There is a cave there, isn't it? I hope it's big enough for us to crawl into. Let's go check it out, Millie."

I was right. Behind the waterfall, we found the entrance to a cave sitting over a ledge jutting out from the rock behind. The layers of sedimentation over the years had formed a sort of natural staircase. This was helpful as the rocks were slippery from the falling water and neither Millie, nor I fancied falling to break our necks on our very first evening out in the rainforest ourselves.

Slowly yet steadily, we climbed upwards mirroring each other's footsteps, already exhausted from our hike and now from our vertical ascend. Millie pulled me up the last few steps and we collapsed on each other laughing and crying at the same time. We had done it! We were going to be fine!

As we crammed ourselves into the enclosure a sense of security fell upon us. It was dusk, and we were tired so setting down the sleeping bags, we huddled close together to ward off the cold; nervous yet excited about our first night in the wilderness. Shadows sulked in the corners of the cave and our echoes ricocheted off the walls, we shifted closer together; grateful we had each other's company and friendship.

CHAPTER 7

Sunlight streamed in from the cracks in the walls of the cave. We woke up, sprawled out on the floor, stretching our limbs.

"You awake?" I yawned though I already knew the answer.

"I think so." She answered. "My legs and arms still feel sore and stiff but other than that I am fine."

We quickly washed up using the fresh water from the river and then whilst Millie packed up the sleeping bags, I opened a tin of canned peaches. We wondered if the teachers and explorers had launched a full search party for us now that we had been gone for a whole day.

Evaluating our next move as we ate, we figured we would follow the river and head Southwest where this habitat's richest biodiversity could be found. Couple of years ago when dad had been gone just a few weeks and his going away wasn't as sore a topic, mum had mentioned his camp was 3°S 60°W sponsored by the Brazil Ecological Conservation Society. Considering that 60% of the rainforest fell within Brazil, we felt confident we would not be breaching any international borders. Millie and I thought we would use our compass to get our bearings and head out immediately so we cover maximum ground during day. Smeared in deet like war paint, ready for our forage into the unknown, we stepped out from the cave that had been our home for our first night alone.

*

Climbing down the rocks proved more treacherous than climbing up had been. We nearly slipped a couple of times, and if the rope we had tied around ourselves hadn't held fast, we would sure have had some very serious injuries. Once on solid ground we walked along the banks, the compass guiding us all the way. At times the river became so wide, we couldn't see the other bank, at times the undergrowth so thick, we had to take big detours, but always the dim of the river, our constant companion telling us we hadn't strayed too far.

I watched Millie, following closely behind her as she kept up a monologue and a steady pace. I felt a rush of affection for this silly girl who had without a second thought to her own safety and the sanity of her family back home, agreed to come with me on this foolhardy quest. Eventually I tuned her and the din of the river out, my mind conjuring up scenarios and speeches of when I would meet my dad. Notice, I say 'when'. I didn't want to think of 'if'.

FLORRRRAAAAAAAAAaaaaaaaaaaaaaaaaa!!

Then...

SPLASH!!!

Snapping out of my daydream, I looked in horror as Millie tumbled into the icy depths of the river. I froze for a millisecond and the next minute found myself jumping in after her. What was I thinking? Or precisely that... I wasn't.

The water hit me like a ton of bricks. Nothing could have prepared me for the onslaught. As I plunged headfirst into the water, I tried to keep my calm but my fear took the best of me. I spluttered and splashed in the most undignified manner. Gasping for breath, I tried to swim towards Millie. I don't know if I've told you but I don't know how to swim very well. So, attempting to do so in the middle of the gushing river, with no adult to help, is very dangerous and ended in an epic failure.

The current dragged me along and I felt as if the rest of the rainforest was oblivious to what was happening to me in its famous meandering river. Blurred images of my surroundings clouded my vision. The constant buzz of the rainforest alternated by the cacophony of the river enveloped me as I struggled to stay afloat despite the river's best attempts to drown me. The forest had me where it wanted me; helpless and hapless; in its clutches.

CHAPTER 8

Through glassy eyes, I saw Millie's head bobbing a few metres ahead of me. Using all of my remaining strength I swam towards Millie, refusing to be separated from her again. It might have been a few seconds but felt much, much, much longer. I kept swimming, refusing to give up.

Aeons later, my hand touched a fallen bough and I held on, literally, for my life. My head went under for a second. When my head resurfaced, I saw Millie had grabbed the other end of the floating bough and now that the gushing river had tamed somewhat, we floated along, taking comfort that we were still together and alive.

As we drifted along, I spotted a few reeds that were doubling over the water. I pointed them out to Millie, and minutes later we were clinging onto them as the rest of the river continued on its journey.

"Now what?" I ask. "We didn't take this into account."

"I suppose we get out of the water and then take stock of our remaining supplies and try and get dry quickly." she added.

Dragging our bodies out off the water, we settled down on the grass, panting and puffing from the effort.

I brought out my backpack and emptied the contents on the ground between us.

"Right. Thanks to my waterproof backpack, we still have my compass, my rope, a fresh set of clothes, my binoculars and … OH NO!", horrified I held up the soggy and damaged illustrated guide in my hand. It was utterly soaked and sodden. "I don't think this can be salvaged?"

"Don't worry. I'm sure I still have mine, I had it in a waterproof plastic wallet. We can use that for our immediate needs. We can wait for the paper to dry for this one and try to iron them together once we get back home." Millie said, before spilling her bag out in front of her.

"NO NO NO." Millie cried. "I don't have my compass or our food rations or my rope!"

"You can use my things and I can use yours." I whispered.

After stuffing everything back, we stood up, hoping to find a clearing and food nearby. We needed to get out of soaking clothes quickly.

Taking extra care while walking now, we consulted the map the explorers had handed out to us. Finally, we emerged into a small clearing where we felt confident, we could build a fire to dry our wet belongings and change into a dry set of clothes. We used this opportunity to reapply some Deet and foot balm which was essential in this hot and humid tropical climate.

Resting and taking turns to turn over the clothes drying in front of the fire, Millie suggested we explore the nearby area for some fruits and berries to eat. We had all but run out of our food supplies. We had only just thought this thought when we heard snickering and short barks behind us and then a small greenish-olive, brownish-grey creature sneaked up and grabbed a few pages of my damaged book right before our eyes.

Following its retreating figure, we saw the most amazing sight ever. Almost as if a fairy god mother watched over us, right in front were several banana trees with fruit as ripe as it possibly could.

Squirrel monkeys sat amongst the branches, happily chomping on the bananas. There was an entire colony of them. "Of course!" I thought. We are close to a river and these playful creatures must be looking for some fun.

I thought they might want to play catch so I threw a rock at one.

It threw a banana back.

It was an Eureka moment for Millie and I. Since we were really hungry, Millie quickly followed suit. Slowly yet steadily our heap of bananas grew larger and larger.

Famished after our ordeal in the river we filled ourselves until we couldn't bear to look at another banana again. Still, we put some in bags for later in case we felt hungry. If I could, I would have kissed these little monkeys for coming to our rescue.

Studying my compass, I pointed us exactly 3 degrees south and 60 degrees west.

And for the second time today, we set off into the unwelcoming depths of the forest.

CHAPTER 9

"**A**AAaaaaaahhhh!!!"

Clearly, I had not learnt anything from Millie's accident earlier today, because if I had, I would have paid attention to where I placed my next footing and would not have ended knee deep in a swamp.

In the background, Millie was shouting "Don't move!" at the top of her voice. "Don't worry! I'm going to get you out. Throw me your rope." Seriously, she must think being stuck in a swamp makes you temporarily deaf.

Between Millie and I, I had the rope in my backpack but trying to get it off myself and to somehow get it out and throw it to Millie made me sink deeper. "Maybe I'll just throw the entire backpack to you?" I asked. "Yessss. just throw the entire thing", she shouted but in the very next breath she said, "no no, just don't move, you're sinking in much faster this way"

As a kid we have played the game of musical statue in several birthday parties but this was the real deal. I stilled my movements as much as I could.

"Now what?" I asked her.

PLEASE STOP moving…, I'll go, I'll get help." She said, nearly in tears. She then pointed at some smoke billowing towards us about a mile and a half ahead to make it more obvious.

And then she was off, her backpack trailing behind her.

It felt absolutely the worst. The swamp crammed itself into every nook and cranny of my body. It's amazing what weird thoughts come to your mind when you're stuck in an impossible situation. Surrounded by murky water, I found myself wishing I was back in the river, its fresh and cold water washing over me. Come on! At least it would have been clean.

I tried to stay as still as possible, fighting the urge to have a full-blown panic attack, training my mind to centre itself. It seemed I had landed myself in an igapo or swamp forest. Seasonal flooding caused large tracts of rainforest to be inundated up to depths of 40 feet. I tried not to think of the worst and prayed with all my might that Millie would find help and return soon.

In what seemed like hours, Millie's figure could be spotted, racing back towards me accompanied with three other people.

Millie and three other men reached me first and boy, was I glad to see them. I thought I noticed one of them slowing down as he approached us but I was too grateful that help had arrived to be really complaining.

By now I was nearly waist deep in the mud.

The first of the men to reach me, asked me to hold the rope they were carrying with them and had flung towards me, as tight as possible. But then the man in the corner, the one that had remained behind and silent all this while, hidden in the shadows, spoke. "Jake, tell her to wrap it around herself and then to tie it around her wrists to be extra secure. Her hands are covered in brackish water and the rope might slip from her grasp."

It was a voice from my past, a voice I recognised, a voice I had longed for two years to hear.

"DAD!!!" I yelled, flinging myself towards him, completely forgetting I needed to be as still as possible.

"PLEASE, calm down miss" one of the men said. His voice sounded urgent so I listened.

Dad continued talking, barking orders, completely in charge. His voice was authoritative and decisive, his orders sharp and precise but his expression deceived him. His eyes twinkled as he spoke and he kept stealing glances at me. It seemed he was as excited to see me as I was to see him. The situation in which we had met, however, was less than ideal.

I tied the rope around my wrist and waited for the men to drag me out. Jake grabbed hold of the rope, giving one end to his friend. "Hold this Matt and pull."

Then the two men, Jake and Matt, yanked at it as hard as they could. The rope coir rubbed against my skin. It felt as if my skin was burning from the friction and the constant scraping.

"STOOOOOP!!!" I screamed. "Please, go slow."

*

At Dad's campsite

After pulling me out, we all trudged to their camp. Apparently falling in the river was a blessing in disguise. Without having to hike all the way, the river had delivered us to our destination, wet and cold and miserable; but relatively unscathed.

Once they settled us girls into our little tent and we had changed and eaten some to regain our strength, dad visited us. Millie gave us our time alone.

"Oh, my darling girl." He cried, lifting me into the air. "Every day, I thought of nothing but you and your mother and your safety."

Though this was pleasing to know, I felt mad. I mean, he did leave us without even saying bye to me.

He leant forward, meaning to kiss my cheek, but I pushed him away, angry he thought he could kiss me after he left us like that.

"What's wrong?" Dad asked concerned.

"Dad, how could you think you could kiss me after you left without even saying bye?" I asked.

"OH." Dad looked at his feet. "I do suppose you're right."

Expecting him to apologise, I put on my 'I forgive you' face. Instead, this is what he said: "How could you be so reckless? Walking into a forest like you own the place. Do you realise the dangers this environment hides? Ever since we heard from your school party and the explorers accompanying that you and Millie have been missing for more than 24 hours, I've been sick with worry"

"You cannot lecture me! You cannot suddenly play parent to me. Trying to find you, Millie and I have run away from our camp, swum against the current in the Amazon river, ran away from a female ocelot and risked disease. To think this is what you say when we finally find you, it's more than disappointing." I shot back.

"That just proves my point Flora!", he retorted.

Tears stung my eyes. "You abandoned us daddy, you abandoned me". I spoke softly through my sobs. Wiping the water from my cheeks, I walked to my makeshift bed and lay down, my body wrecked with sorrow and disbelief, my mind consumed with anguish and anger.

And then, the merciful escape of sleep.

CHAPTER 10

The beautiful dawn chorus stirred me awake and I felt as if I was in heaven. The harmony of the chorus was like natural instrumental music.

Dad's figure loomed over me and his face had a concerned expression painted all over it.

"Are you okay?" he asked. "As I understand it you cried yourself to sleep".

"I am fine." I retorted.

"I am not comfortable with the way we left things yesterday and I wanted to make up it to you by taking you and your friend on a tour of the area we are studying." Dad said.

"That sounds nice." I whispered. Unexpectedly, (for him and me) I launched myself on him, hugging him tight, breathing in his familiar smells.

I told Millie about this tour and she wholeheartedly agreed to come with us.

*

Dad and I were standing outside mine and Millie's tent in silence as we waited for her to get dressed to join us.

"So, what are you going to show us?" I asked. I had been pondering over this question all morning but hadn't managed to get a believable answer.

"If, I told you it wouldn't be a surprise and I want it to be one." Dad laughed. He seemed relieved I was talking to him again and I suddenly felt ashamed of my little speech.

Millie had come out of her tent and we were ready to go. We walked from the tents to the section of rainforest dad and his colleagues were studying. My jaw dropped. The view was absolutely magnificent.

It was without any question, the best day of my life. We saw every inch of the area of study, some places even twice! We saw boa constrictors, sloths, toucans, golden mantilla frogs, golden tamarin monkeys, blue morph butterflies, tree and glass frogs and even caught a glimpse of a harpy eagle. However, the boa, the harpy, the golden tamarin monkey, the glass frogs and the golden mantilla were my favourites.

Dad led us through the areas he 'knew like the back of his hand'. "Oh loooook!" Millie drawled, pointing to a nearby tree. A huge snake lay draped across a low branch.

"The Boa constrictor." Dad muttered. Then louder he said: "Do NOT disturb or startle her. She is our most fascinating study. Did you know Boa constrictors also have two lungs, a smaller left and an enlarged (functional) right lung to better fit their elongated shape, unlike many colubrid snakes, which have completely lost the left lung. There are currently 10 recognised subspecies of boa constrictor. Boas are not venomous. They kill their prey by constricting it (squeezing it so that it can no longer breathe), before swallowing it whole. That is why they are called boa constrictors."

"In school we learnt about the rainforest and these are some facts I remember: the bigger the snake, the bigger the prey it will attempt to catch. Larger boa constrictors may even take monkeys or an occasional deer. A Boa is NOT the largest snake in the rainforest even though it is quite big. The green anaconda is significantly larger." I added. "Oh my god. I feel like a know-it-all."

"Yeah, yeah everyone knows." Millie snickered.

Next, we saw a harpy eagle.

"She looks like she is eating so we should leave." Dad said looking worried. "Though she's eating now, she can attack and severely injure us if threatened."

"Ok." We replied, moving away from the harpy. We walked further into the jungle, oohing and aahing at the extraordinary flora and fauna in the rainforest.

"Girls. Look!" dad exclaimed.

I turned my head to see what he was looking at. I almost didn't see it.

"Look closer." Dad whispered.

Millie was nodding her head in agreement. Obviously, she had already seen what dad was showing us.

"Oh. Hang on a sec. Yes. I see it, I see it." I said, looking triumphant.

"isn't it a glass frog?" I asked.

"Yes, and it's called that because it's skin is transparent like glass." Millie replied and the proceeded to rattle off some amazing facts about it.

I turned around to see she had her guide out and was reading off it. "Hey! No fair!", I scolded her playfully.

We had so much fun the day simply flew by. Soon it was time to return to the camp. I was elated having found Dad. I walked smiling to myself, reliving the mad adventure we had had and how Millie and I had found him. It was almost unreal. As we were walking, I suddenly remembered Dad having said something about receiving information of us missing from our teachers.

"Dad?" I asked softly, "you said yesterday that the school group got in touch with you after we went missing? What was that about?"

"Oh. Your friend saw you sneak off when you went to the toilet and told your teacher. Then your teacher used the satellite phone to get in touch with us since we have been here for a while and fairly familiar with the area. They have a search party going, as did we ever since we found out. I have been besides myself with worry".

"Uh oh." I said, just as Millie said "Whaaa... Who?"

"A really sensible young lady called Fiona Groves? Yes, I think that's her name" dad replied.

The stares I had felt on my receding back as I had raced towards the toilets had been real. I looked at Millie and she looked at me quizzically. "I'll explain later", I mouthed back.

Dad was still talking and what I caught was "... basically your entire group is coming here to take you home tomorrow", he finished.

"But but but... Mr. Maxwell, how did they ever know how to contact you?" asked Millie, speaking my mind.

"Well, at any given time, there could be a few groups of researchers in the rainforest. The Brazil Ecological Conservation Society has been here for a few years now and we are also quite well known amongst researchers. It was natural for them to contact us if their students went missing. As far as their travelling here is concerned, it was anyway planned for the end of the trip, in fact it got delayed because no one knew which direction you both went in. Since we found you, we have been in touch with local authorities and your school group to let them know you're safe and sound. They should be here by midday tomorrow."

I swear, if looks could kill, Millie would have murdered me a HUNDRED TIMES over by now.

Aaah, best friends!

*

Dusk.

Dad had said his goodbye and we had parted ways; he went off to his tent as we trudged the last few steps to ours, practically falling into our sleeping bags. I filled Millie in with what had previously felt like a figment of my imagination, or at best an unimportant detail. Now it turned out, it was quite an important detail. Fiona was only the most annoying person in the world.

"To a successful mission." Said Millie

"To a successful mission." I repeated.

"Goodnight."

"Goodnight."

CHAPTER II

"**M**illie... Millieeeee." I whispered. Shaking her side to side, I tried to rouse her awake. "Wake up you sleepyhead."

"Flooora!!!" Millie moaned. "You just had to wake me, didn't you? Ooooh... I was dreaming of being back in my house with my family and my beloved pooch"

"Listen Mill" I repeated. I pointed to the flap of our tent.

"Yes, yes. I do suppose you're right Mr. Maxwell. We'll have a stern word with the girls but nothing more, I understand your family's special circumstances and also appreciate all your help here. Had it not been for your research group's willingness to assist, we may never have found them. Oh! how dreadful that would have been, I shudder to think."

Where had I heard that voice before? Oh yeah! Our teacher, Mrs. Caesar. They were already here. We must have slept most of the morning away.

"Let's hurry." Millie commanded. "Get changed and, let's head out together to meet them.

"Millie, I don't feel comfortable leaving dad so soon... I barely just met him again", I muttered in a low voice.

"Flora, my sweet friend, you've found your dad now. He's not going away. You've proven to him the lengths you will go to have him in your life and I don't think he's going to abandon you like this again. Let's go out and when you get a moment alone, speak to him. I say communication is the key."

"Now, dear girl, I've stayed away from my comfort zone for a long time for you, now you do that for me. Come on, it may not be your strong point, but we have got to face the consequences of our actions", Millie scolded. Then she added: "Sorry. I didn't mean to be that harsh."

"It's cool. I know what you mean. And you're right"

We quickly got dressed and hurried out of our tent.

I went rigid. My heart stopped beating if only for a second. My skin prickled as I now faced what I always known would happen; yet denied; at the end of this food hardy quest. I could no longer push it to the back of my mind, it was real and it stood in front of me in the towering form of Mrs C.

"GIRLS!!!" screeched Mrs. Caesar. "You are alright. Oh, I've been beside myself with worry." We could barely breathe, enveloped by Mrs Caesar into a massive hug. We looked at each other. This was unexpected, and umm… nice.

"Mrs C, we can't breathe". I said, trying to shrug her off. I stole a glance at dad and found him shaking his head disapprovingly. I tried to mouth we were being squished in a death grasp but dad gave me a quizzical look when I did, so I stopped.

"Yeah, we're ok." I said looking down. Millie was looking so happy, still enveloped in her hug.

"We're really sorry Mrs C, we didn't mean to worry you or the other adults. We, we, we... we got carried away" she said sheepishly.

"We'll talk about that at length later girls. You have some serious explaining to do and we need to re-establish what are acceptable and unacceptable boundaries. The Principal will talk to you about that. But for now, I'm just happy to see you're both safe.

Now, your friends and classmates await you. Let's go and meet the group.

In the evening your father's team has kindly offered to set up a bonfire for us. Isn't that amazing? How does hot cocoa with marshmallows, followed by dinner sound, hmmm?" Mrs. Caesar asked.

"That sounds lovely. Thank you." Millie said, looking directly in to the teacher's eyes.

Millie had always been a teacher's pet. Now was no exception.

"Oh, my dear girls..." Mrs C enveloped us once again in her warm embrace and this time we hugged her back.

*

Dusk.

The whole class sat, gathered around the wooden logs burning in the middle. Conversation had broken all around.

Around and around.

Easy, comfortable banter.

Over hot cocoa and marshmallows followed by a hearty meal of soup and bread, chicken sandwiches and cookies, we talked. Mostly about the adventures Millie and I had had since we went missing from the group. Our friends and classmates told us what they had been up to, other than organizing search parties to look for us. Some seemed jealous of our adventure, some angry that their trip had been short circuited, others just happy to see us.

Looking at this, a warm fuzzy feeling slowly crept up on me. These were my friends, this was my tribe, these are the people that mattered. I saw the faces of my near and dear ones, aglow from the reflection of the fire. Dad was talking to Mrs. Caesar. Millie with some other friends. I suddenly missed mum, thinking how she must have felt hearing the news of me going missing. I wondered if Dad had called to tell her we had been found and we were safe.

Mental note to self: Check with Dad if Mum knew about our little adventure.

CHAPTER 12

Last day at campsite

"Flora. Flora. Wake up, my darling girl. We need to talk and I'd rather do it before anyone else wakes up." Dad hissed.

Yawning, stretching my limbs, I rubbed my aching neck muttering, "Must have slept in a wrong position or something".

"Hey! I'm still talking, wh… where are we going?"

Leading me outside, dad ushered me into a quiet corner so we could talk in peace.

"Listen." he whispered urgently. "I've finally mustered up the courage to speak to you. Please hear me out before interrupting." He took a deep breath and then continued. "I know it was wrong to leave you like that, alone and confused. I know I should have explained my actions and my absence. I had a reason. I promise I did. At that time, it seemed like a really good one. Now of course I understand that it wasn't. You see my darling, me and your mother were facing marital discord, irrefutable differences and … well let's just say we were both not in a good place emotionally and mentally. We tried really hard to work at it, we visited several counsellors and sought help. Eventually, we decided to… uhh… how should I say it… well, take a break.

That made me angry, albeit, unreasonably, so I left and came here. I used this research project to bury my anger and immerse myself in work so I could take my mind off whatever was going on between your mother and I.

I am only now realising that I made a grave mistake. I should not have run away from my personal problems and most definitely not left like that without even a good bye to you. I want to make amends. I really do.

I hope you will understand that adults too can make foolish, rash decisions at times. I hope you can find it in you for forgive me.

Now that you are aware and you're also old enough to offer a mature point of view, let us discuss together, all three of us, how we want this relationship to work out.

Now you can ask your questions." He finished, breathless yet almost relieved he had gotten it all out.

"Dad why can't we go back to normal as one big happy family? Why can't you both live together?" I whined.

"Sweetheart, I don't know how to answer that. All I know is that that might not be possible. I'm sorry. I know it must be hard for you."

"I am not sure I do understand, but I can definitely try. Thank you for trusting me enough to tell me the truth." I spoke softly.

*

Goodbye.

I didn't know I hated goodbyes.

As much as I had craved for a goodbye when he left home, I was dreading it this time. Researchers, teachers, students, friends and classmates clambered aboard the coach from our base camp. Chatting and twittering, pairs sat down, excited from the adventurous trip they had had and longing for the lazy, familiar comfort of their home. Making certain to sit right at the back, Millie had saved me a place beside her.

I stared out of the glass pane window, unabashed, unblinking and utterly devastated. A lone figure stood outside staring right back at me, his eyes bearing a million unspoken promises.

"I'll be back dad." I vowed as the coach began to drive off.

*

AFTERWARD

"**M**ummmm....!" I called down the stairs. "Could you get me a torch for the trip? Pleeeease." I add because I know mum is a strong believer in magic words.

"Sure thing, sweetie." Mum replied and soon after I heard a loud thump as she closed the door behind her.

Now that Mum was gone, I could start my packing.

100 hours of community service for Millie and I for risking our lives and disappearing, 3 months of being grounded by mum and extra credit work for our zoology submission; we had finally redeemed ourselves. The restrictions had finally been lifted and I was packing my backpack to go to the Amazon Rainforest, this time, as a welcome guest not a rebel on a mission.

"All set." I thought, "All set!"

Printed in the United States
by Baker & Taylor Publisher Services